Let's Explore
Deserts

Tammy Gagne

Wonder Books
An Imprint of The Child's World®
childsworld.com

Published by The Child's World®
800-599-READ • childsworld.com

Photography Credits
Photographs ©: Ray Redstone/Shutterstock Images, cover (background), 3 (background); Steve Byland/Shutterstock Images, cover (coyote), 1, 3 (coyote), back cover; Milan Zygmunt/Shutterstock Images, 2, 14–15; Dmitry Pichugin/Shutterstock Images, 4, 4–5; Sean R. Stubben/Shutterstock Images, 6, 11; Danita Delimont/Shutterstock Images, 7; Red Line Editorial, 8; Hagit Berkovich/Shutterstock Images, 12; Pablo Garcia Saldana/Shutterstock Images, 16; Roger Clark/Shutterstock Images, 19; S. Borisov/Shutterstock Images, 20, 20–21; Nesolenaya Alexandra/Shutterstock Images, 22

ISBN Information
9781503857971 (Reinforced Library Binding)
9781503860308 (Portable Document Format)
9781503861664 (Online Multi-user eBook)
9781503863026 (Electronic Publication)

LCCN 2021952373

Printed in the United States of America

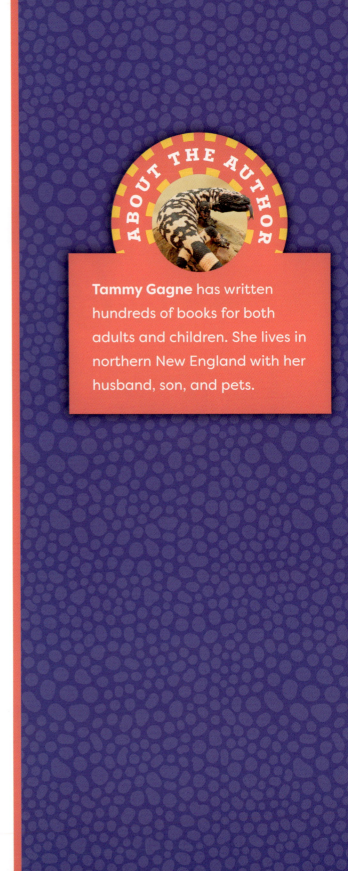

ABOUT THE AUTHOR

Tammy Gagne has written hundreds of books for both adults and children. She lives in northern New England with her husband, son, and pets.

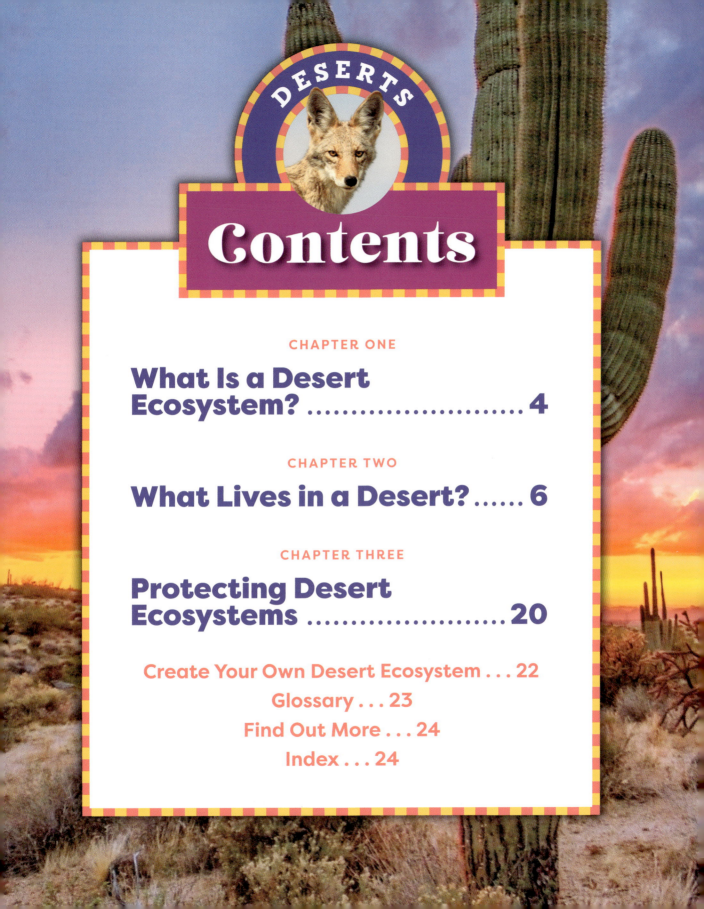

Contents

CHAPTER ONE

What Is a Desert Ecosystem?

Deserts are the driest places on Earth. They get less than 10 inches (25 cm) of **precipitation** each year. Deserts are found on all seven continents.

Some deserts are the hottest places on Earth. The Sahara Desert in Africa gets as hot as 122 degrees Fahrenheit (50 degrees Celsius). Other deserts are cold. The world's largest desert is in Antarctica. Temperatures there can drop as low as –129 degrees Fahrenheit (–90 degrees Celsius).

Desert plants and animals are used to the dry conditions. They depend on each other to survive. Together, they help the **ecosystem** succeed.

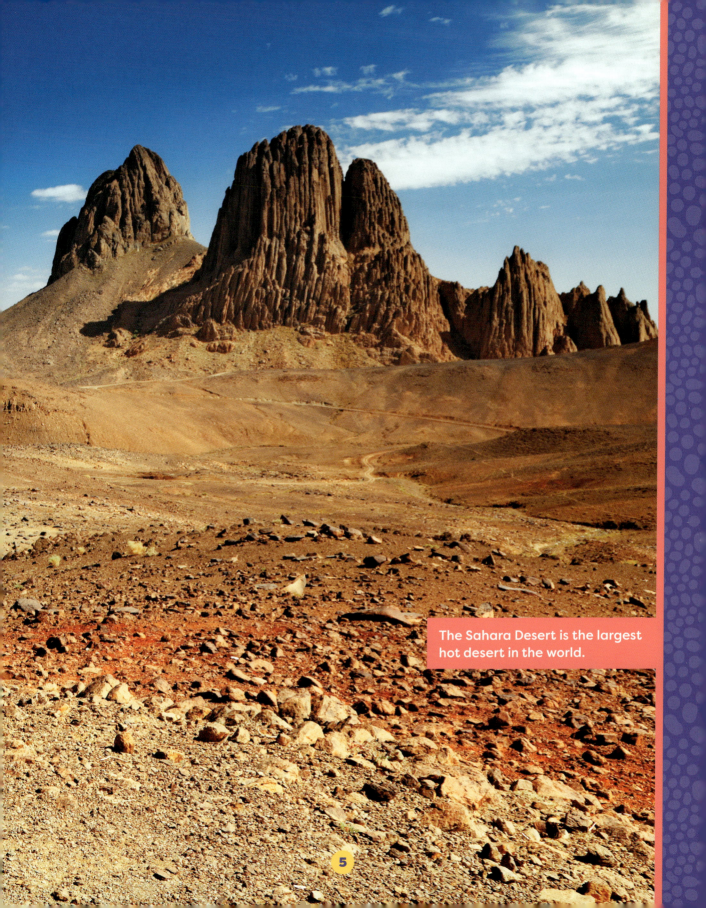

The Sahara Desert is the largest hot desert in the world.

CHAPTER TWO

What Lives in a Desert?

SAGUARO CACTI

One of the biggest desert plants is the saguaro (sah-WAH-roh) cactus. It only grows in the Sonora Desert in Arizona. Saguaro cacti can grow up to 40 feet (12 m) tall. It takes about 200 years for a cactus to reach that size.

The plant's roots collect water whenever rain falls. The cactus stores this water. It has thick and waxy skin. The skin prevents the water from being absorbed by the hot air.

The saguaro cactus uses the water to make fruit. Animals such as bats eat the fruit. The cactus has thousands of spines. The shade from the spines protects the cactus from the harsh sunlight.

The saguaro cactus does not have very deep roots. Instead, most of the roots are as wide as the cactus is tall.

Bats spread saguaro seeds in their waste after eating the fruit. This carries the seeds to new places.

DID YOU KNOW?

EARTH'S LARGEST DESERTS

Deserts

Deserts can be found all over the world. Many deserts are hot, but a few are cold. This means very different kinds of animals can be found in deserts.

GIANT DARNER DRAGONFLIES

The giant darner dragonfly lives in the deserts of the southwestern United States and Mexico. Its wingspan can reach 5 inches (13 cm). The giant darner is a desert **predator**. It eats many smaller insects such as flies and mosquitoes.

Young giant darners are not picky eaters. They will even eat other young giant darners. This helps the **species** survive when food is hard to find.

The giant darner also serves as **prey** for larger animals. Birds and frogs eat them.

CACTUS WRENS

The cactus wren is a bird found in the deserts of the southwestern United States and northern Mexico. It eats insects, fruits, and seeds found on the ground. Sometimes it will even eat small frogs and lizards. Cactus wrens serve as food for larger predators. Bobcats, coyotes, foxes, and hawks all hunt these small birds.

Water is limited in deserts. But the cactus wren can survive without drinking much. Instead, it gets most of its water from the food it eats. Cactus wrens lay more eggs when there is a lot of food. They lay fewer when food is hard to find. This makes it more likely that their young will survive.

Cactus wrens often live in areas that have cacti, such as prickly pears, and thorny shrubs.

Fennec foxes dig tunnels underground to stay in during the day. These tunnels help them avoid the heat.

FENNEC FOXES

The fennec fox lives in the Sahara Desert in Africa. This species has large ears. Its ears help it stay cool. The fennec fox also uses its ears for hunting. It can hear prey moving underground.

The fennec fox digs into the sand to hunt rodents and insects. The animal helps nearby farmers when it hunts rodents. When there are too many rodents, they can destroy crops that feed humans.

Fennec foxes also eat birds, fruits, and leaves. Fennec foxes even hunt prey bigger than themselves, such as rabbits.

Fennec foxes are the smallest fox species. Even the biggest ones weigh just 3 pounds (1.4 kg). But they play a big role in their ecosystem. Without fennec foxes, prey populations in the Sahara would grow too large.

GILA MONSTERS

The Gila (HEE-lah) monster is a lizard found in the southwestern United States and Mexico. It eats lizards, birds, frogs, and other small animals. The Gila monster kills its prey with a strong and **venomous** bite.

Gila monsters do not spend much time hunting. They do not need to eat very often. Gila monsters can go months between meals. Gila monsters also drink as much water as they can whenever they find it. This helps them survive long periods with no rain.

These lizards spend most of their time underground. This helps keep them safe from predators. Coyotes, foxes, and badgers all hunt Gila monsters. But the Gila monsters can fight back. They use their painful bite.

Gila monsters cannot see very well. They hunt by using their senses of smell and taste.

Gila monsters store large amounts of fat in their tails. Their bodies survive on this fat between meals.

DID YOU KNOW?

15

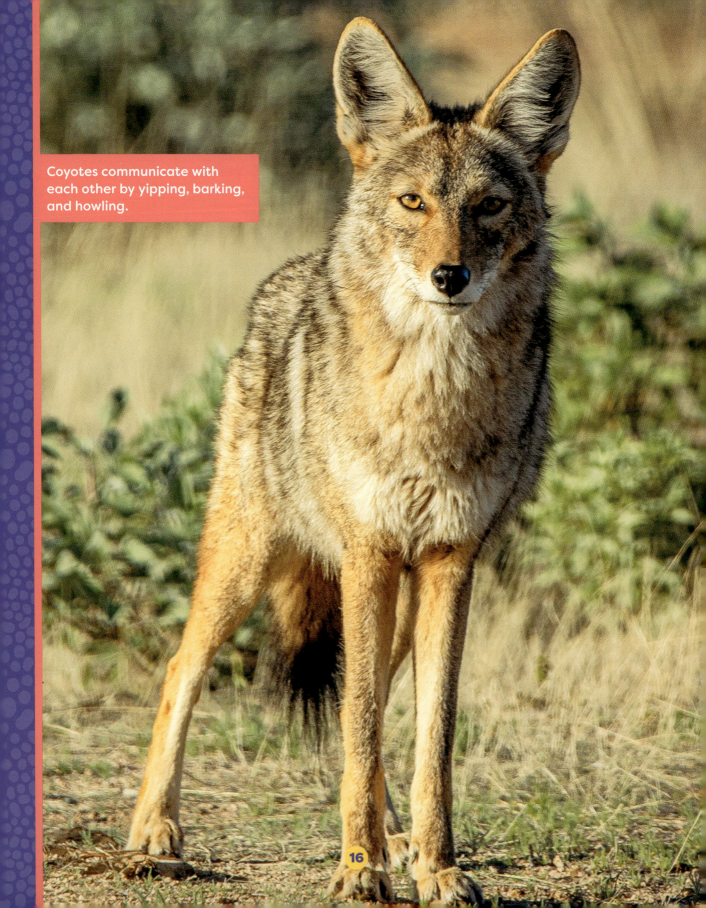

Coyotes communicate with each other by yipping, barking, and howling.

COYOTES

Coyotes are important desert predators. These doglike animals are skilled hunters. They eat small animals such as mice, rabbits, and squirrels. These prey animals multiply quickly. By hunting them, the coyotes help keep their numbers in balance. Coyotes hunt other desert animals, too. These include foxes, raccoons, and skunks. By hunting many types of animals, coyotes keep the wildlife in deserts balanced. No population gets too large or too small.

Coyotes are not large animals. Most coyotes weigh between 20 and 50 pounds (9 and 23 kg). But a coyote can hunt a deer. Sometimes they hunt in packs. They work together to take down bigger prey.

Coyote howls can echo. This makes it sound like a pack is bigger than it really is.

DID YOU KNOW?

EMPEROR PENGUINS

The emperor penguin lives in Antarctica. Temperatures get extremely cold on the continent. But this penguin has layers of feathers. They overlap to protect the penguin from the cold and Antarctica's strong winds. In addition, the bird has a large amount of fat. This also keeps it warm.

Emperor penguins leave land to search for food. They eat fish, squid, and krill from the ocean. The birds spread important nutrients between land and sea through their waste.

Emperor penguins are an important food source for other Antarctic animals. Large birds such as southern giant petrels eat emperor penguin chicks. Adult emperor penguins serve as food for larger animals such as leopard seals.

Emperor penguins are the largest penguins. They can grow to be 4.2 feet (1.3 m) tall.

CHAPTER THREE

Protecting Desert Ecosystems

Some desert ecosystems need people's help. Many deserts have gotten hotter in recent years because of **climate change**. This has made it harder for some animals and plants to survive.

Sometimes humans threaten desert ecosystems. Hunting and construction disrupt life in deserts. Some animal populations have dropped to dangerous levels. These species should not be hunted. Many people have also built entire communities in deserts. Many animal habitats have been destroyed in the process.

Humans can help solve these problems. They can stop building in deserts. And they can work to stop climate change.

Climate change is causing some deserts to grow hotter and drier. This makes it harder for plants and animals to survive.

Create Your Own Desert Ecosystem

Desert plants have adapted to survive without much water. You can create the right conditions to grow a desert plant.

Materials
- Sand
- Dirt
- Bowl
- Jar with a lid
- Rocks
- Succulents or other desert plants
- Water

Directions

1. Mix sand with a little dirt in a bowl. You will need enough of the mixture to fill several inches of your jar.

2. Pour the dirt and sand mixture into the jar.

3. Plant the succulents or other plants in the jar.

4. Next, carefully surround the plants with rocks.

5. Pour ½ cup of water into the jar.

6. Close the jar. Place it in a sunny spot.

Glossary

climate change (KLY-muht CHAYNJ) Climate change is the human-caused change of Earth's weather patterns and climate. Climate change is making deserts even hotter.

ecosystem (EE-koh-siss-tuhm) An ecosystem is all of the living and nonliving things in an area. Deserts are a type of ecosystem.

precipitation (prih-sih-pih-TAY-shun) Precipitation is water that falls from the sky to the Earth in the form of hail, mist, rain, sleet, or snow. Deserts receive very little precipitation.

predator (PREH-duh-tuhr) A predator is an animal that hunts and eats other animals. A coyote is a predator.

prey (PRAY) Prey are animals that other animals hunt and eat. Emperor penguins are prey for larger animals.

species (SPEE-sheez) A species is a specific group of living things that has the same features. Fennec foxes are the smallest species of fox.

venomous (VEN-uh-muhs) Something is venomous if it can poison a living creature. The Gila monster has a venomous bite.

Find Out More

In the Library

Roumanis, Alexis. *Deserts*. New York, NY: Weigl, 2018.

Walker, Alan. *Food Chain in a Desert*.
New York, NY: Crabtree Publishing, 2021.

Weglinski, Michaela. *In the Desert*. Washington, DC:
National Geographic Kids, 2020.

On the Web

Visit our website for links about deserts:
childsworld.com/links

Note to Parents, Teachers, and Librarians: We routinely verify our Web links to make sure they are safe and active sites. So encourage your readers to check them out!

Index